Christmas At
Stony Creek

Christmas AT Stony Creek

BY Stephanie Greene

PICTURES BY

Chris Sheban

Greenwillow Books
An Imprint of HarperCollins*Publishers*

Christmas at Stony Creek
Text copyright © 2007 by Stephanie Greene
Illustrations copyright © 2007 by Chris Sheban

www.harpercollinschildrens.com

Book design by Paul Zakris
The text type is 18-point Venetian 301

Library of Congress Cataloging-in-Publication Data
Greene, Stephanie.
Christmas at Stony Creek / by Stephanie Greene; illustrations by Chris Sheban.
p. cm.
"Greenwillow Books."
Summary: With her father away and her brother injured, it is up to little Pip to find food
for her hungry siblings and mother mouse, but it is a hard winter and the only place
where she is likely to find Christmas dinner is at Land's End, where the people live.
ISBN-13: 978-0-06-121486-8 (trade bdg.) ISBN-10: 0-06-121486-8 (trade bdg.)
ISBN-13: 978-0-06-121487-5 (lib. bdg.) ISBN-10: 0-06-121487-6 (lib. bdg.)
[1. Survival—Fiction. 2. Family life—Fiction. 3. Hunger—Fiction. 4. Mice—Fiction. 5. Christmas—Fiction.]
I. Sheban, Chris, ill. II.Title.
PZ7.G8434 Chr 2007 [Fic] 22 2006050984

First Edition 10 9 8 7 6 5 4 3 2 1

 Greenwillow Books

For George, who always had faith in Pip

—S. G.

Contents

Christmas at Stony Creek

chapter 1

✳ Pip, Short for Pipsqueak ✳

They roasted the last chestnut the night Papa left home.

He sat in his chair in front of the fireplace with Nibs and Nan tucked in on either side. Mama knitted in her chair across from him, her foot rocking Baby Finny asleep in the cradle.

The three older children sprawled on the floor. The glow of the fire flickered over their faces. Will, with his injured leg, stared silently into the flames.

Kit lay beside him, whittling his newest carving.

Pip was the one with her head in a book.

Pip was always the one with her head in a book.

"Better look sharp, Pip," Papa warned in his deep voice as he cracked the warm chestnut open, "or the greedy beggars you call your brothers and sisters won't leave you a crumb."

"When is a mouse a bookworm?" said Kit. "When her name is Pip."

"Pip's a worm. Pip's a worm," chanted Nibs and Nan, and giggled.

Pip looked up at her father and smiled. He was the one who had named her Pip, short for Pipsqueak, when she was born.

"You were so small we made a nest for you in a

teacup," he told her, again and again because she never got tired of hearing it. "We thought we had lost you until we heard a tiny squeak and saw two huge brown eyes looking up at us."

Pip was still small. She was quiet, too. It used to be that she was sometimes lonely in the midst of her boisterous family. She felt as if no one saw, or heard, her. Then, one day, Papa said, "You may not speak in a big voice, Pip, but I hear you, loud and clear."

Pip never felt lonely again.

"It's all right," she told him now. "I don't like chestnuts that much."

Papa knew she didn't mean it. Everyone in the family loved the dense meat of the glossy nuts. They were a special treat. But there had been so few of them this winter. So little food of any kind.

Pip would be glad to give her share to Will if it would help bring his old smile back.

"Nonsense," Papa said. He held the shell with the meat cut into equal pieces out to her. "There's plenty to go around."

Pip took a morsel and held it up to her nose. The rich smell made her empty stomach grumble. She tucked it into her pocket for later.

Papa looked around at his family, his kind face wreathed in a reassuring smile. "I'll be home in two days with more food than you've ever seen," he said. "Three days at the most. We'll have a Christmas feast. Invite everyone we know."

"Hip, hip, hooray!" squealed Nibs and Nan.

Papa tickled them, making them shriek with delight. Then Mama took them off to bed. Soon it was Pip's bedtime, too.

"Your brother may need your help finding food while I'm gone," Papa said as he tucked the blankets snugly around her. "This snow is giving his leg a devil of a time."

I can't! Pip wanted to cry. *You have to be strong and brave to find food! I'm afraid!*

She longed to ask Papa about the spots of blood she had seen dotting his paws when he came home from digging for food in the deep snow that had covered the woods for weeks.

And about the stories she had heard of the hungry animals roaming through the trees, stealing any food you were lucky enough to find.

The look she saw in her father's eyes stopped her.

"Don't worry, Papa," she said. She patted his huge paw with her tiny one. "If Will can't do it, I can."

"I know you can, my girl," Papa said. He kissed her and stood up. "You can do anything in the world."

Pip clutched at a corner of his jacket. Papa was like a tall and gentle giant. Her very own gentle giant, who kept her safe.

"Three days at the most?" she asked.

"Three days at the most," he promised.

chapter 2

✳ When Will Papa Be Home? ✳

ip, come back!" the other skaters called. "Come back!"

"I can't," Pip cried. "I'm late!"

She tucked her chin into her chest and ran. The wind sliced through her thin coat. Sleet pricked her face like icy nails.

The last light of the day was fading from the sky.

Pip never should have stopped to skate. She should have found food and gone straight home. But

it had been so wonderful to glide and twirl across the pond, to whip around at the end of a long chain, happy and carefree like the tail of a kite.

To forget, even for an hour.

Pip had been having so much fun she hadn't realized the time. Now she was late. Mama would be worried.

And all Pip had found for dinner were a few seeds and a small piece of corncob.

She started up the hill in front of her. The thin layer of ice covering the snow made the going treacherous. Suddenly Pip slipped and banged her head. Tears rushed to her eyes.

Oh, *where* was Papa? she thought, as she struggled to her feet. Why didn't he come home? Three days had become eight, and there was still no word from him.

And where was Will? Why wasn't he helping her?

He was the oldest. And the bravest.

At least he used to be brave. But not anymore.

Not since his trip to the house perched at the edge of the cliff, overlooking the woods. Land's End, it was called. Will had gone there with Uncle Hank last fall.

When he came back, he was changed.

He dragged his wounded leg behind him. He jumped every time he heard a loud noise. Will, the family joker, no longer laughed.

And Uncle Hank was dead.

Pip gave herself an angry shake. What would Uncle Hank have said if he had seen her standing here, crying? What about her promise to Papa?

Pip struggled on.

The sleet-covered snow made the going treacherous. For every two steps she took forward, she slid one step back. *Oh, why didn't you bring your walking stick?* she scolded herself fiercely. *You'll never get home at this rate.* The thought brought a sob to her throat.

Then miraculously, through the gloom, Pip spotted a patch of bright green against the white. It was the tip of a Christmas fern, poking its head through the ice. Pip grabbed it and pulled herself forward.

There was another fern, and another.

Slowly she inched her way to the top of the slippery bank. A small, round window nestled in the roots of a tree was straight ahead. It was lit by a single candle.

Home.

Pip's heart soared as she ran toward it. She could hardly wait to get inside. She'd throw herself into her mother's arms and ask the questions that had been running through her mind all week. *Where's Papa? Why doesn't he come back?*

What if he's dead, like Uncle Hank?

Mama would tell her not to be silly. She'd say nothing would ever happen to Papa. That he'd be home tomorrow, for sure. They would feast on barley soup and hot corn fritters.

Everything would be all right.

The comforting warmth of home wafted over Pip's face as she opened the front door. She heard her mother's anxious voice.

"Where have you been, Pip?" she called. "I've been worried sick."

And Pip knew that everything wasn't all right, after all.

"Sorry, Mama!"

Pip hung her wet scarf on a peg beside the door and curved her mouth into a smile. Then she closed the door and shut out the night.

chapter 3

✳ "I'm Still Hungry" ✳

'm still hungry," said Nibs.

"Me, too," said Nan.

"Here. Have mine." Pip pushed her plate across the table. "I've had enough," she lied.

Next to them, Will was eating with his head down. Kit was busy licking his plate.

Finny pounded her cup on her high chair. "More! More!" she squealed.

Her sweet face was so indignant Pip had to laugh.

"Now, you hush." Mama came out from the kitchen and stood wiping her paws on her apron as she looked around the table. "That's all the food there is. You should be grateful for it."

"I know where there's more," Kit said in a low voice.

"Kit . . ." Mama said quietly.

"I do," he insisted. "And *I'm* not afraid to go there."

"That's enough!"

Mama's sharp voice echoed around the room like a shot. Nan and Nibs froze. Kit lowered his plate silently to the table. Only Will kept eating, bowing his head even lower.

The rest of them stared at their mother, astonished.

Mama never raised her voice to them. Never.

"If anyone says another word about food, I don't know what I'll do," she said. Her voice was shaking.

No one said a word until Finny started to cry. The sound unfroze them all.

Mama scooped Finny out of her high chair and carried her from the room. Pip stood up quietly. "Let's do the dishes," she said.

Will pushed his chair away from the table and limped into the living room without looking back. Nan, Nibs, and Kit followed Pip into the kitchen.

When the dishes were washed and put away, Pip helped the little girls into their nightgowns and read them a book. Then she went into her own room and shut the door. Her walking stick was lying in its place on the floor beside her bed. Pip picked it up.

It was her special stick, long and straight, with a fork at the top like a Y. Uncle Hank had helped her make it last summer.

He had shown Pip how to peel off the bark to reveal the slippery, silky wood underneath. How to sand it over and over again until the sharp knots became smooth humps and the stick was as smooth as glass.

It looked delicate, but it was strong. Uncle Hank said there wasn't another stick like it.

"It's hickory wood," he told her as he turned it over in his gnarled paws. "Nothing's stronger than hickory. This stick will come in mighty handy, you'll see."

He was right.

It had saved Pip from falling into Stony Creek when she slipped on Twig Bridge during the flood. It was the perfect thing to use when she played the proud king in games with Nan and Nibs. It had helped her scare off nasty Badger when he poked his nose into her hiding place during a game of hide-and-seek.

One sharp *rap!* had sent him running.

Uncle Hank never knew how right he had been, but Pip thanked him silently each time she felt the stick's smooth strength. She ran her paws along it now as she thought about what Kit had said at dinner.

She knew where she could find more food, too.

At Land's End. The people had built it last

summer, cutting down trees and destroying the homes of countless animals to make room for it.

Pip had never seen it, but she'd heard stories.

The people who lived there had more food than they could eat, everyone said. They covered their tables with food. What they couldn't eat, they threw into huge metal cans with locks.

It was hard for Pip to imagine such riches. Having so much food you would throw some away.

Uncle Hank and Will had gone up there to see it for themselves. When Will came back alone, Mama had made the rest of them, including Papa, promise they wouldn't go near it.

Promising had been easy for Pip. She never wanted to *see* Land's End as long as she lived. But in the quiet of her room, holding the stick that gave her strength, she knew she might have to break her promise.

If she didn't go, Kit would.

Pip couldn't bear it if something were to happen to her other brother because she was afraid. If her father didn't come home soon, she knew she would have to go.

chapter 4

✳ Two Days to Christmas ✳

T he sleet had stopped during the night. The morning sun ricocheted off the thin coat of ice that covered the ground, the rocks, the trees. The whole world glittered.

Christmas was two days away. Pip didn't know how they could celebrate it without Papa.

"We have to, Pip," Mama told her after lunch, while the twins and Finny were taking their naps. Pip and Mama were baking cookies with the nuts Mama

had saved for Christmas sweets. "The twins would be so disappointed if we didn't. Imagine what Papa would say."

Mama's voice was firm. "We'll go ahead and decorate the tree. We'll plan a wonderful day. Papa will be home just in time, you'll see."

She took Pip into her bedroom and showed her the acorn rattle filled with pebbles she had made for Finny. And the rag dolls for Nibs and Nan.

Their button eyes didn't match, and their bodies were flimsy from lack of stuffing. Pip knew her sisters would love them all the same.

"Papa finished Will's flute before he left," said Mama, "but I don't have anything for Kit. I was hoping you could find a stick for him. Teach him how to make one the way Uncle Hank taught you."

Pip's heart sank. More than anything, she wanted to stay home. To be there when Papa arrived. But she couldn't let her mother down.

"I can do that," she said. "It would be a wonderful present for Kit."

"I knew I could count on you." Mama gave her a quick hug. "I'll finish the cookies myself," she said. "Go now! You'll have to hurry if you're going to find a stick and be home before dusk."

Pip got her own stick and went outside. It would be hard to find the right piece of wood with so much snow and ice, but she knew exactly where to look.

"Down at the bend in Stony Creek, where it branches off toward Silvermine Road, that's the spot," Uncle Hank had told her as he led her down the hill that day so long ago. "There's an old shagbark hickory there. Got hit by lightning about ten years ago. Most folks think it's dead, but it's just fooling."

Remembering the way he had chuckled made Pip smile.

"Folks came and got the nuts, but they left the most valuable part," Uncle Hank said. "Hickory wood's hard and strong. You remember that, Pip."

Yes, that was where she would go, Pip decided as she poked her stick through the icy snow. Maybe she'd find some dried berries on the blueberry bush she passed along the way. A treat for Nibs and Nan.

But there was someone she needed to visit first.

chapter 5

✳ One Step at a Time ✳

"A unt Pitty, are you there?" Pip scratched lightly on the door hidden in the bank in front of her. "It's me, Pip."

"Why, of course it is," a friendly voice said as the door creaked open. "Who else would it be?"

Pip was wrapped in a soft embrace that smelled of apples and cinnamon. When Aunt Pitty finally held her out at arm's length, the loving face of the old rabbit was creased in a welcoming smile.

"I haven't seen you in weeks," said Aunt Pitty. "You're as skinny as a willow whip. Come in and let me get you something to eat."

She drew Pip into the warren and shut the door. Pip rested her stick against the wall and followed Aunt Pitty down a dry tunnel to the kitchen.

"Of course, I haven't been outside much myself lately. My rheumatism's been acting up something terrible. Sit down, while I get you some apple cobbler." Aunt Pitty bustled around the cozy kitchen while she talked. "There isn't much, but I'm glad to share. Terrible winter, this. If it goes on much longer, I don't know what we'll all do."

She put a large bowl on the table in front of Pip and sat down across from her.

"But you know that, don't you?" she said, looking at Pip closely. "Eat, and tell me about the family."

Aunt Pitty had known Mama and Papa since long before Pip was born. She'd known Uncle Hank, too. She was the one who had come over to straighten Will's leg after the accident.

Aunt Pitty listened carefully as Pip told her about Papa.

"Eight days, you say?" she said when Pip was through. "Well, it's a long way, Pip, even in fine weather. I bet your Papa has found himself so many good things to eat, dragging all that goodness back home is what's taking so long. Yep, I reckon that's it."

"Do you think so?" said Pip. "Do you really think so, Aunt Pitty?"

"Yes, I do," Aunt Pitty said firmly. "And I suggest

you think the same. It doesn't do a body any good to think the worst."

She got up stiffly and went over to the counter to pull out a deep drawer. "Now, how's the family set for food?"

"There's hardly anything left," Pip said. "It's up to me now, because of Will's leg. But he's so much better at finding it than I am."

"Nonsense," said Aunt Pitty. "You're as capable as anyone. It's all in knowing where to look. Have you tried the banks along Turtle Pond?"

"Yes. There's nothing left."

"Hmm, how about Hollow Log? No, that's no good. That greedy Badger told me he'd picked it clean." Aunt Pitty sniffed. "Laughed about it, too."

She was busily stuffing things into a burlap bag. "I can give you some seeds and some berries," she said, "but I'm clean out of nuts of any kind."

"But what about you?" said Pip. She longed to ask Aunt Pitty about Land's End but didn't dare. Aunt Pitty would tell Mama for sure.

"Don't worry about an old rabbit like me. I hardly eat anything these days." Aunt Pitty put the sack on the floor next to Pip's chair and rested her warm paw on the top of Pip's head. "You just have to keep digging and scratching," she said, looking into Pip's eyes. "Even if it takes all day."

"It's hard," Pip said in a small voice. "Sometimes I'm afraid."

"We're all afraid of something," Aunt Pitty said

kindly. "No one's expecting you to turn brave overnight. Braveness is earned one step at a time, Pip. The first step's usually the hardest. Don't give up. You'll get there."

Aunt Pitty settled herself into the chair beside the wood-burning stove and patted her lap. "Now, come over here and sit for a bit. Aunt Pitty will sing you a song."

Pip climbed gratefully onto Aunt Pitty's lap and snuggled down.

Maybe she would never have to take the first step, she thought. Maybe she could stay here, safe and warm, until Papa got home.

Pip closed her eyes and listened.

chapter 6

✳ Owl! ✳

"Pip, wake up."

Pip reluctantly abandoned the warm comfort of sleep and sat up. "Is it Papa?" she said, rubbing her eyes. "Is he home?"

"No, it's not Papa." For a minute Aunt Pitty's kind face looked sad. Then she smiled. "You slept for an hour," she said. "You'd better get going. It gets dark awfully early these days."

Pip followed her back down the tunnel to the door.

"Take good care, now," said Aunt Pitty, winding Pip's scarf around her neck. "Don't let this beautiful day trick you." Pip grabbed her stick as Aunt Pitty held open the door. "Remember," Aunt Pitty said, "everyone out there is as hungry as you are."

"I'll be careful," said Pip.

Aunt Pitty's sack was a reassuring weight against Pip's back as she hurried down the slope to Stony Creek. She followed the creek past the deer beds for a while, making sure she stayed hidden in the bushes.

When she reached the crooked bend in the creek called Old Man's Leg, she saw what she had come for. The huge shagbark hickory was lying on its side. Its gnarled branches sticking out of the snow waved to her like fingers.

Pip's spirits soared as she ran into the clearing. All caution was left behind. She didn't sense the danger until a shadow swept across the sky. Something dark and dangerous glided over her head.

Owl.

Wasn't it too early for him to be out? Pip thought, looking wildly for a place to hide. It must be what Aunt Pitty said. Owl was as hungry as everyone else. And Pip was a delicious morsel.

Oh, how could she have made such a foolish mistake?

She was out in the open with no place to hide. The terrible sound of heavy wings was all around.

The smell of her fear filled the air.

Pip spotted a tiny hole in the ice straight ahead. It

was her only hope. She hurled the sack to one side and heard the seeds and berries scatter across the ice as she started to run.

The deadly swoosh of Owl's wings came closer and closer. Pip dived toward the hole with a sob of relief.

It was blocked.

A thin sheet of ice lay across it like a cruel joke. It was the only thing between her and safety. Pip raised her stick over her head and brought it down with all her strength.

The sound of shattering ice mingled with Owl's screech as she slipped into the hole. Owl's talons closed on empty air inches above the ground.

She was safe. Pip hugged her stick to her side as

she lay there, panting. *Thank you, Uncle Hank. Thank you.*

As Owl's angry voice faded in the distance, Pip's heart slowed and became calm. When all was quiet, she poked her head out of the hole and looked around.

The sack was lying empty on the ground.

Only minutes before, it had been so full. Pip crawled out of the hole and picked up the limp sack as gently as if it held a sleeping baby.

Because of her, Aunt Pitty's precious gift was gone.

What would Aunt Pitty think of her? And how could she bring herself to tell her mother what she'd lost? Pip realized then what she had to do.

chapter 7

✳ "It Was the Trap" ✳

That night, when everyone in the house had gone to bed, Pip crept quietly into Will's bedroom. "Will," she whispered, "are you awake?"

She climbed onto his bed and felt her way along it in the dark until she came to his feet. He was lying on his back, staring into the night.

"I'm awake." Will's voice was flat.

Pip drew her legs up inside her nightgown for warmth. "I need to know about Land's End,"

she said softly. "You have to tell me."

"I don't want to talk about it."

"But you have to. It's the only place left," Pip said. "There's lots of food at Land's End, isn't there?"

For a minute she thought he wasn't going to answer. Then, "Mountains of it," Will said in a reluctant voice. "Crumbs under the table . . . crusts between the floorboards . . . dried bits of egg stuck to the seats of the chairs—"

He stopped.

"I have to go up there. You know I do." Pip's voice was calm. "Tomorrow is Christmas Eve. We don't have anything to eat."

Will was quiet.

"You need to tell me everything," Pip said fiercely.

"Where to go. What to look for. About Cat."

She stopped. She had never asked Will this question before. "It was Cat who killed Uncle Hank, wasn't it?"

The room was so still she heard someone moan in her sleep on the other side of the wall. Nibs, maybe. Or Nan.

"No, it wasn't Cat." Will's voice was barely a whisper. "It was the trap."

Will started to talk.

He told her how quiet and strange the huge kitchen had felt in the moonlight. How he and Uncle Hank had started across the floor, searching for crumbs. How they'd heard a noise and started to run for cover under a cupboard.

Suddenly Uncle Hank had stopped. "He told me to go on," Will said in a whisper. "He said he would be with me in a minute." Will's voice broke.

"Shhh . . ." Pip patted his feet the soothing way Mama would have done. "Hush," she said. Will was quiet for a minute, and then he started again.

Uncle Hank had turned and headed off toward the windows, alone.

That's when a movement caught Will's eye. Cat was crouched in the doorway, ready to spring. Before he could cry out a warning, Will said, a deafening noise filled the room.

A trap rose into the air as its jaws snapped shut.

There was a cry from their uncle.

Then silence.

"I ran." Will's voice was full of shame. "When Cat's nails sank into my leg, I thought I'd never see home again. Then Uncle Hank gave one last cry, and Cat turned. He let me go. Uncle Hank saved me, Pip," Will said in a hushed voice. "I made it back through the crack in the wall and onto the porch."

Will's voice stopped. Pip was almost afraid to breathe.

"I can't go back there," he said. "I can't."

"That's all right." Pip looked up at the window. She could see the moon shining down through the branches of their tree. "I'm not afraid to go by myself," she said.

She wished in her heart that it were true.

chapter 8

✳ "I'll Go Tonight" ✳

It was Christmas Eve. The house was filled with the smell of pine. Pip and Kit had dragged home all the pine branches they could find. They draped them over the fireplace. They hung them from the doorways. They spread them, soft and thick as a carpet, along the hall.

The tallest bough, they declared, would be their tree.

Nan and Nibs were decorating it now. They hung

ornaments, oohing at their beauty. They tossed tinsel, giggling when it missed. They chattered back and forth while they worked, their tiny eyes sparkling with excitement.

Finny stood in her playpen and laughed.

Mama had saved a bit of flour and some raisins. While the little girls took their naps, she baked a Christmas cake and hid it in the cupboard. It was smaller than any cake they ever had before, but still, it was a cake.

"What will we have for Christmas dinner?" Nan said, jumping up and down. "Will we have cakes and puddings and sweets?"

"Will this be the best Christmas ever?" cried Nibs. "Will it, Mama? Will it?"

"Hush, you sillies." Mama laughed and swept them up in her arms. "It's a surprise, you know that."

"But what if Papa isn't here?" asked Nan, suddenly serious.

"We can't have Christmas without Papa," said Nibs.

Pip felt the sudden sting of tears. She draped her last bough over the mantel. She wiped her eyes.

"I'll go call Will for dinner," she told her mother quickly. She let herself out of the house and ran down the path to Stony Creek.

Will was coming toward her as fast as he could, dragging his leg behind him.

"Great news, Pip!" he called. "The people are gone! They're not there!"

He was out of breath when he reached her side. "I was talking to Squirrel, you know Squirrel, he knows everything. He told me the people have gone away for Christmas. Isn't that wonderful?"

"But there won't be any food if they're not there," said Pip.

"Sure there will," Will scoffed. "People leave it all over the place. They never clean it up. There will be plenty of food. And no Cat." He said the words slowly, saving the best for last.

"No Cat?"

"Squirrel said the people sent him to a place where he'll be taken care of while they're gone. Big bully can't even take care of himself."

"Oh, Will, that means it's safe!" cried Pip.

"As long as you don't touch the trap," Will warned. "But you'd better get up there soon, before the word gets out."

"I'll go tonight."

"Promise me you won't go near the trap."

"I promise."

"No matter what?"

Pip looked back at him with shining eyes. "No matter what."

chapter 9

✳ Pip's First Step ✳

T he bowl Pip was drying slipped and fell to the floor with a clatter.

"What's wrong with you tonight?" Mama asked. "That's the second dish you've dropped."

"It's Christmas Eve," said Pip. She picked up the bowl and put it carefully on the shelf. "I'm excited, that's all."

"Are you sure you're feeling all right?"

"I'm fine. Really." Pip ducked her head to avoid

her mother's worried look. All she wanted was for the evening to be over and everyone to be in bed.

When Finny began fussing in her high chair, Mama went to comfort her. The twins came and leaned against Pip.

"When's Papa coming home?" said Nan, tugging at the hem of Pip's skirt. "We never have Christmas without Papa."

"Will we still get presents if he isn't here?" asked Nibs.

Pip picked them up and carried them, squirming, to the fireplace. "Why, what else do you think you're getting for Christmas?" she said, sitting in Papa's chair with one on either side. "Papa, tied up in a red bow!"

The little girls giggled.

"He isn't a present," said Nan. "He's our papa."

"Yes, and we can't dress him up and play with him," added Nibs. "Besides, we're getting dolls."

"Because that's what we asked for," finished Nan.

"Come along, girls," Mama said from the doorway. "If you don't go to bed now, you'll be too tired to play with those dolls, won't you?"

"I'm going to bed, too," said Pip. "Good night."

She brushed her teeth and slid under her quilt, still in her clothes. She could hear Mama singing to Nibs and Nan as she tucked them in, then saying good night to Kit and Will.

Mama came into Pip's room last. Pip held her covers tight under her chin when Mama sat down on the edge of her bed.

"I want to thank you for being so grown-up about Christmas," Mama said. "You've never complained about having to do Will's job or not getting enough to eat. When Papa gets home, I'm going to tell him how brave you've been."

"I haven't done anything brave," said Pip.

"Sometimes keeping your fears to yourself is the bravest act of all," said Mama. She kissed Pip's cheek. "Good night, Pip."

"He'll be home tomorrow," Pip said when her mother reached her door. "I know he will."

"Yes, and it will be the best Christmas ever," said Mama. "Just as Nibs said."

Across the room they looked at each other and smiled.

chapter 1 o

✳ Land's End ✳

t was cold and very late.

Mama had sat up in front of the fire for a long time. Pip had had to pinch herself to stay awake. The clock in the dining room was chiming midnight before she finally heard her mother's bedroom door close.

Pip hopped out of bed, grabbed her stick, and crept down the hall to the front door. Will was already there.

"Be careful," he whispered as he held the door open. "Don't forget your promise."

"I won't," said Pip. The door clicked quietly behind her.

She stood stock-still in the night. She strained her eyes to see, her ears to hear.

Not a footstep. Not a sound. Even the wind was asleep.

She looked longingly at the round window behind her. She thought about her family, warm and safe in their beds. And then she thought about Papa.

Was Papa safe and warm tonight? Or was he alone, cold and hurt?

Pip drew a deep breath and held her stick more tightly against her.

If Papa could be brave, so could she.

There was no more time to waste. Pip scurried from rock to bush. From bush to log. Hiding, ever hiding, from eyes in the night. The air smelled clean and cold. *I can do this,* Pip thought. *I can!*

She ran faster and faster without making a sound, never staying in the open for long. She didn't see another living creature the whole journey. Finally, she came to the stone wall that marked the end of the woods and the beginning of the huge field she would have to cross.

Pip saw it the minute she reached the top of the stone wall.

Land's End.

It towered over the horizon, its blank windows

staring down at Pip like empty eyes. Pip looked ahead at the steep hill she would have to climb and shivered.

"You'd better hurry if you want to get anything." Pip's heart gave a great leap as Squirrel jumped up onto the wall next to her. "I saw the rats from North Woods heading that way," he said. "They'll take it all."

"They can't," Pip cried. "It's mine!"

"I wouldn't try telling them that if I were you," said Squirrel. "A tiny thing like you is no match for them."

"Tiny can be good," Pip said defiantly, drawing herself up. "Tiny can be brave."

"I certainly hope so, for your sake. Good luck!" Squirrel called as he ran off into the woods.

Pip started across the field.

The food's ours, she thought as she ran. *Nibs's and Nan's. Finny's. Kit's. Will's. Greedy rats aren't going to take it from us. I won't let them.*

Pip didn't think about Owl. She ran.

Dried stalks stuck up through the snow, casting ghostly shadows. Craggy heaps of dirt, dumped by careless bulldozers, rose in front of her like mountains. Up and down, around and around. *Use your stick, Pip. Keep going. Don't give up.*

By the time she reached the bottom of the hill, Pip was panting and exhausted. And oh, what a hill it was.

Jagged rocks jutted from its steep side like rows of unfriendly teeth. The wind had blown away the snow to reveal frozen dirt. There was no grass. No trees. Only a few sad roots, few and far between, for her to cling to.

Pip didn't know how she would make it. Then she heard Aunt Pitty's voice. *Braveness is earned one step at a time.*

Pip began to climb.

Her feet slid on the slick dirt. Clumps of coarse bush loomed in front of her. Pip jabbed her stick into the hill, again and again. She pulled herself around every root, each bush. One step after the other, she climbed.

Jab, pull. Jab, pull. Rest.

Jab, pull. Jab, pull.

When she reached the top, she threw herself onto the flat ground with a sob. She'd made it. She crawled gratefully forward and looked up.

She was lying at the bottom of the porch steps.

They stretched as far as her eye could see. At the top the porch sat empty and serene. Waiting.

Pip slowly stood and walked forward. She reached out to touch the bottom step. It was covered with a layer of slippery ice. All the steps would be covered with a layer of slippery ice.

All the way to the top.

Pip grabbed the edge of the bottom step and tried to pull herself up. She slid back. She tried again. She slid back.

It was too slippery. She would never make it.

Climb the lattice. The soft voice whispering in her head was Will's. *The lattice will be easier,* he had said.

Pip ran around to the side of the house. Lattice was nailed to the steps so animals couldn't crawl underneath. Pip saw the narrow boards, nailed together in a crisscross pattern, with friendly little spaces between them she could grab on to and pull. She took a deep breath and started to climb.

First this way, then that. Grab here, put your foot there.

Slowly Pip crisscrossed her way to the top and slipped over the edge onto the porch. She had made it. And there was the wood box on one side of the door, the way Will had said.

Pip slipped behind the box and in through the crack between the edge of the door and the house and looked cautiously around the strange place she had entered.

Huge and silent, the room was as chilly as a tomb.

Wooden cabinets rose to touch the ceiling high above her head. A table with four chairs stood in the middle of the floor. The refrigerator hummed; a clock ticked.

The room was empty.

Pip ran along the molding under the cabinets. Will had told her that was where she would find the most crumbs. Sniffing and running, sweeping her whiskers across the floor, she ran the length of one wall.

There was nothing.

She ran up and down the cracks between the floorboards.

Nothing.

She scrambled up onto the kitchen counter.

Nothing.

She squeezed in behind the stove and jabbed her stick into the greasy darkness.

Still nothing.

Will couldn't have been wrong. He couldn't.

Pip ran faster and faster, searching. Again and again she ran under the cabinets, her ragged breath echoing in the night.

It was no use.

There wasn't a single crumb. The wonderful things Will had told her she would find were gone.

The rats must have gotten there first.

Pip huddled in the middle of the empty floor and cried. She was a tiny mouse in a huge, empty house, alone.

She had failed.

chapter 11

✳ It Might Just Work ✳

The full moon moved slowly across the windows. The faucet dripped rhythmically into the white sink. Pip didn't know how long she had been lying on the floor. It was so strangely peaceful she felt as if she could lie there forever.

Suddenly her nose twitched.

What was that?

Pip sat up and sniffed the air.

What *was* that? she wondered. Then she saw it,

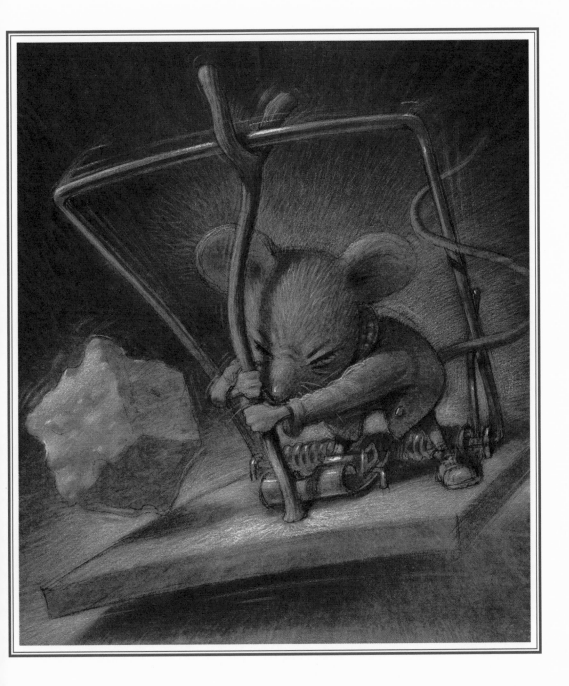

tucked into the murky corner on the far side of the room beneath the windows. Hidden in the darkest shadows, waiting.

The trap.

Pip moved slowly toward it, as if in a dream.

It was bigger and more awful than anything she had imagined. Its powerful jaws were open wide, terrifying and patient.

She knew she should run now. But she couldn't. Pip had seen the intoxicating prize the trap held for her, if only she were brave enough to grab it.

It was a piece of cheese.

The most magnificent piece of cheese Pip had ever seen. The closer she got, the more the smell of it filled the air like perfume.

Beads of fat twinkled on its waxy surface like stars.

It was huge.

Huge enough to feed her entire family for weeks.

All the promises Pip had made to Will disappeared like the cloud of her own breath in the chilly air. She couldn't go home without it.

She circled the trap slowly.

Will had told her how it worked. How, if you lifted the cheese, the platform it was sitting on would move, making the vicious jaws slam shut with a speed no mouse could outrun.

Pip closed her eyes. She wouldn't see Uncle Hank's body trapped there; she *wouldn't*.

There had to be a way.

If only she could stop the trap from springing. If

only there were some way she could stop its jaws from snapping shut.

Think, Pip, *think.*

She rapped the end of her stick angrily against the floor.

Suddenly she stopped.

That was it.

You won't find any wood stronger than hickory. Hickory'll hold up anything.

Pip held her stick out in front of her as if she were seeing it for the first time. She looked at the trap, then back at the stick.

The trap. The stick. The trap. The stick. Her mind raced as her eyes moved thoughtfully back and forth between the two.

She leaned the stick to the left.

To the right.

She traced the path of the steel jaw in her mind again and again.

It just might work. As terrifying as it was, she had to try.

Then the most terrifying thing of all happened. Night became dawn.

Its pale light streamed through the windows and moved slowly across the floor, as unstoppable as the tide. If Pip didn't act now, she would be caught in the house in the clear light of day. Would have to make her way back across the field. Anything could see her and catch her.

Pip felt strangely calm.

Moving slowly, taking care not to jiggle the trap, she rested the end of her stick on the spot where the jaws would hit. She twisted it slowly until the Y was in the right position.

There was nothing more she could do.

If it didn't work, she would die.

If she waited another minute, she would lose her nerve.

Pip took a deep breath and flicked her long, delicate tail around to tap the platform holding the cheese.

Whap!

The steel jaws slamming shut filled the room with a mighty roar. The stick held.

It stood there quivering in the early-morning light

under the weight of the steel jaws, and it held.

Pip had done it.

Quickly Pip dragged the cheese off the trap and pushed it across the floor. She threw the weight of her body behind it, squeezing it through the crack onto the porch.

"Pip!" Will's cry was joyful. "You're all right!"

"Look, Will," she said. "Isn't it beautiful?"

Her eyes opened wide.

Will was standing on the porch of Land's End.

He'd come back.

"I had to," Will said, as if reading her mind. "You were gone for so long. I thought you were dead."

They looked at each other without speaking. Then Will grinned his old grin. "We'd better get going.

We're going to catch the dickens when Ma finds out."

Will reached into his jacket and pulled out a piece of vine. He and Pip tied it around the cheese and dragged it to the top of the stairs.

"Look out below!" Will shouted.

The beautiful cheese, huge enough to feed a family, tumbled down the steps. They pushed it to the edge of the hill, and it tumbled all the way to the bottom. Pip and Will ran after it, laughing, and grabbed the end of the vine.

The sky was getting brighter, but a light snow had started. It fell around them like a veil, protecting them.

The cheese glided easily over the crusty snow as they ran across the field. When they got to the stone wall, Pip scrambled to the top. She pulled while Will pushed. They leaped to the ground and pulled the cheese down after them as they ran into the woods.

Something landed on a branch above their heads. A shower of snow cascaded around them. "Good for you!" Squirrel shouted. He chattered and chirped. "Merry Christmas to you and your family!"

"Merry Christmas," Pip whispered. She didn't dare shout.

On they ran.

Will was limping now, but they didn't stop.

Not until they saw the round window snuggled in the roots at the base of the tree, lit by a single candle.

They were home.

chapter 12

✳ The Best Christmas Ever ✳

ama!" Pip cried, throwing open the door. "Look what we have!"

Her mother appeared in the living room door. Tears were running down her face. "And look what I have, Pip," she said.

Pip was wrapped in strong arms that smelled of Papa.

"Where were you?" she said, pressing her face into his broad chest.

"I made a foolish mistake and spent a few days in a deep well," said Papa. He held her out to look into her eyes. "Don't tell me you doubted me for a minute."

"Never," Pip whispered.

"Will, my boy." Papa slapped Will on the shoulder and pulled him close. "Where on earth did you find such a feast?"

"Pip found it," said Will. Nibs and Nan were watching the cheese with awe. Kit licked his lips and eyed it greedily.

"No food just yet, Kit," Papa said. "Let's go into the living room. These two are soaked through."

Papa led Pip over to the fire. Mama wrapped her and Will in blankets. Kit, Nibs, and Nan crowded around, as close to their father as they could squeeze.

Mama sat next to him with Finny.

They were all laughing and talking at the same time. Finally, Papa said, "Quiet now, all of you. It's time for Pip to tell us her story."

From the safety of her father's lap, Pip told them. No one said a word until she got to the end. "Will helped," she said. "I couldn't have done it without him."

"That was nothing," said Will. "You wait until my leg gets better."

"But, Pip," Mama said in a quiet voice, "you lost your beautiful stick."

"It doesn't matter," Pip said. "I'll make another one. I'll show Kit and Will how to make one, too. I can make one for everyone, can't I, Papa?"

"You can do anything in the world, Pip," he said. "It's always been so."

Nibs and Nan leaped up and twirled around the room, giddy with happiness. Nan ran to her mother.

"Are we having the best Christmas ever, Mama?" she asked. "Are we? Are we?"

"I think maybe you should ask Pip."

Nan threw herself across Pip's lap. She gazed up into Pip's face with eager eyes. "Are we, Pip?" she pleaded. "Are we?"

"Yes, we are," Pip said. "The best Christmas in the world."

✳ Postscript ✳

he lights in the kitchen at Land's End went on. Footsteps sounded across the floor.

Then: "Philip?" The woman knelt. "Come, look at this."

There was amazement in her voice.

The man came over and stood next to her. Then he knelt too. "What in the world . . ."

Together, they stared at the wondrous thing in front of them.

It was the trap.

Its jaws were held open by a slender, smooth hickory stick shaped like a Y.

The cheese was gone.